WATERMAN

THE LEGEND OF EVOLUTION

SCREENPLAY

WRITTEN BY

WINS DEUS

WATERMAN

WATERMAN'

'WATERMAN' is the story about a MAN who travelled oceans of time to find his love and then take revenge on his enemy , Frankenstein.

This story is about a man called Dharamputra…who lived his whole life on an island in the middle of the sea with his wife. After spending 20 years of their life they had a son with extra ordinary features which enabled him to survive under water as well as on the earth. He looked like a   fish in a man's body and was given the name "Water man."

One day Waterman meets a girl called "INDIRA", who is a student of arts…she comes to the island with a bunch of people and somehow   loses her way back home. Indira falls in love with Water man and tells him about the world which exists beyond the island. Water man's imagination about the world starts spinning in his head. One fine day, they get an opportunity to move from the island and see the world, with the help of Water man's water creature friends like whales and other creatures , they cross the volcano surrounding the island

This story is also about a scientist called Bhishamacharya and his student Shelly, who found the formula to create "Frankenstein.". After years of research in the biological field to make a dead person alive with modern technology…they created Frankenstein and other creatures. Frankenstein could not be controlled by any one. Before finishing the entire process, Frankenstein kills all the other creatures and escapes from the lab.

This story is about the villain… created by a human, who challenges nature and finally got what he deserved from the society and nature. This story is about an adventures man "WILLIAM". Who spent his whole life to find the criminals of society, whether it was Water man or Frankenstein..

This story is about a Mermaid called "WATER GIRL" the daughter of Water man and Indira, who fights for her survival and the rights she deserved being a living creature on this earth, and taken care by Shelly who is responsible for all the un wanted things which happened to her. This story is about a man who suffered for his love and struggled his whole life to save the people from the man made dragon "FRANKENSTEIN.." This story takes you to a world where nature can save humans and their earth but when we go against its principles, it can destroy the stability of human survival.

ONE LINE

Story begins with scientist Bhishamcharya and his assistant Shelly (Mary)…who is a foreigner…and having a degree in biology. They create a flying horse and many creatures which are against nature, with their special formula, That formula and technology lead them to give life to a dead human… and they start the process of FRANKENSTEIN… before finishing the process **Frankenstein** blasts… destroys all the creatures and escaped from the lab.

20 Years Later

"INDIRA", who gets an unexpected opportunity to meet her daughter, from the investigation officer (nick named Sherlock Holmes) "WILLIAM". He led her to "SHELLY", the Director of HUMA special creatures caring center, in France. Shelly is taking care of Indira's daughter for past   20 years.
Year 2014…

In Paris HUMA was protected by heavy digital security to protect Water girl… and Indira was welcomed to see her daughter.   After meeting Shelly… Indira came to know that she is the mother of the girl who can't survive on the earth. She was suffering for last 20 years under   the water and was given the name "WATER GIRL".
Water girl is going through a critical condition, which can lead to her death. When Water girl comes to know about her mother she gets curious to know

about her past life. Meanwhile some incident cures her decease and this miracle makes   history in medical science.
Shelly arranges full security around Water girl… despite that Water girl gets kidnapped by an unnatural

creature.

Investigating officer William inquired and starts his mission to get back Water girl.

1000 km. from France (in Alps) some terrorists are planning to destroy the diversity of India "Taj mahal".

"FRANKENSTEIN" lands from the sky to misty mountain, holding Water girl in his hands. His landing makes earth crack. Which make terrorists scared and lead them to fight with Frankenstein.. In between the fight Frankenstein lost water girl. Frankenstein kills half of the terrorists and searches for Water girl.

William accompanied by one of his subordinates Ajay and air force officerrs were searching for water girl with the help of satellite. Because of misty and snowy mountain it was hard to see anything. They land their helicopter and start looking around. William reaches the terrorists dead bodies which lead him to find Water girl, who is under the water in the sea.

"WATER MAN" riding a whale like horse…from sea to sky…to reach Alps with the help of the signal which all the water species have, to save his daughter Water girl from Frankenstein..

On the way to save water girl, an distraction from the terrorists… made him to save Tajmahal.

Shelly in the helicopter accompanied by soldiers… reach Water girl to take her back to the lab.

Shelly and water girl leave in one helicopter followed by William and Ajay in another helicopter. Frankenstein who is hiding nearby attack William's helicopter and pulls it down in the sea… under the water. Frankenstein fights against many whales… he killed them all and escaped.

With the news of… Taj mahal saved by some strange person… Indira had assurance that Water man is alive'.

Shelly insists Indira to talk about her past life… Water girl can't understand the language… to make water girl understand Shelly asks Indira to tell the story through micro phone, which will help Water girl   understand about her mother and father's life.

20 years back…

Indira is a student of College of fine Arts… she used to see a particular dream of a strange person who lives in the middle of the sea. This dream inspires her to paint a painting of her dream…which got so much appreciation from her professors and all students.

At the end of the year of their degree, the college planned a world tour.

In the middle of their world tour, Indira's boyfriend Manish with his group planned to go to Volcano Island, which is near Africa. On the way to Volcano Island, the volcano erupted and a cyclone sank their boat in the sea. Somehow few of them reached the shore of the sea and some died on the way including Indira's best friend Mansi.

Indira realised this is the same Island which she used to see in her dreams… she gets curious and went into the forest to see the place, which was confusing her- whether she was dreaming with open eyes or it was real. She reaches a cave which looks strange than what she saw in her dream. She spends hours in this cave then suddenly realizes that she is alone there and has to return to be with her friends.

Manish with all his friends search for Indira all around, but couldn't find her and finally they left from the Island, with the support of the navy.

Indira reaches the shore and sees the boat leaving. It has already gone too far from the island… she tries to call them but no one could   hear her voice.

    Indira slept off on the shore… next day she woke up with the same unbelievable dream which she was seeing for the last few years… A strange man riding a whale in the sea and coming towards her… she opens her eyes… it was not a dream but real, she was shocked and wanted to escape from there, she fell unconscious near the shore.

Water man comes near, lifts her up and attends to her and she awoke.

Water man is also scared to see a human.. so many years of his life living on the island without ever have seeing another human being… Many days Indira suffered without drinking water and food, at last she needs Water man's help, than she came to know… for last 20 years he was staying alone in this cave and cannot speak any language.

Gradually they came to know each other and fell in love.

Indira taught him how to speak…and asks about his life… Water man takes her to a cave which was in the shape of human sculpture… and the whole cave was carved with text… she read and came to know… 52 years back after Indian freedom South Africa was suffering from poverty and disease… a writer named Dharamputra came along with his friend to find out their difficulties and wrote a novel on their life.

One of the photographers lead him to see the burning Volcano and the Island where no human lived for last few centuries. After reaching there, their boat sank…his friend died and he couldn't go back.

He lived many years on the rock in the middle of the sea.

    Many months later… he found some dead bodies around the rock… one was alive, which was a Russian girl. They lived together for 20 years, after that the water level went down and they could see the island near. There they had a child… who is "WATERMAN".

After giving birth to Water man… his mother died and after five years his father died. Water man takes Indira into the cave and showed his god and goddess which are his mother and father… decorated with corals and flowers.

Water man took Indira to see the whole island and Volcano. They reach the other shore of the Island… suddenly Volcano erupted and there were land slides too. It was a horrible condition for her to live like this, and she decided they had to leave this place to lead a normal life, where she came from.

One day some pirates came to the island to hide some of their precious cargo. Indira sees them and thinks that this is the right opportunity to escape from the island. While asking for help from the pirates some accident happened which killed all the pirates. Indira and Water man go with the boat and   reach the normal world.

This place was full of lights… which Water man had never seen in his life, it was a galaxy for him.
Water man doesn't know this galaxy is inviting him for some unfortunate situation in the shape of a scientist Bhishmacharya and Shelly's miracle Frankenstein..

Indira left water man on the shore and went to buy some clothes and something to eat for both of them.

A monster Frankenstein. in the shape of a man appears and starts killing the people around the shore and disappears. Water man is waiting for Indira to come, this blame of killing all the people goes on to Water man, he hid himself under the sea and police arrests Indira. On the way to the police station, Water man appears and fights with police and takes Indira along and hides in the ship to set sail for   India.

Frankenstein had already reached India before Water man. Frankenstein.'s full body is hurting because of the unfinished process of scientist's miracle. He is suffering from the pain, this pain leads him to go against all the humans until he gets his success on the land.

International police satellite find Water man and Shelly and put them behind the bars. The nation was against Water man and decided he should be hanged till death.

Frankenstein   still continue with killing people in the city, Water man and Indira came to know about Frankenstein and they escaped from the jail to prove themselves innocent.

William… the officer of special crime branch, understood the innocence of Water man and Indira and that there is another Water man who is doing all the crime or maybe he is a vampire.

Water man reaches Frankenstein with his special abilities and with the help of   all the species to find this different creature.

William follows his satellite to find the one who is doing all the crime.
Countless people dying every day… even animals, everywhere silence, India slept for days.

Indira wants to save Water man by proving his innocence… William wants to destroy the person who is destroying the world.

Water man finds Frankenstein… Fight between them leads Water man to death under the sea… Indira was watching him die but couldn't do anything to save him. William wanted to save Water man but William is no match for Frankenstein… so he couldn't do anything but watch. William takes Indira along to save her from Frankenstein. This incident made Indira go out of her mind…

Present…

Indira finishes telling her story… Water girl gets very emotional after listening to her mother's story.

William appreciates her courage and congratulates her for being a very good and famous painter in France and her contribution to art.
Shelly who created Frankenstein… not to harm anybody but to keep alive her lover Victor who died in an accident… with the help of medical science she could make him alive… but before she could finish the process…Frankenstein got wild. This experiment made her to face the judgment... and cause of Water man's death. Indira lost her life and mind which lead her to mental asylum for many years.
Shelly…who was unintentionally responsible for all… has given the job to take care of Water girl.

Frankenstein, is looking for his creator Shelly to take revenge for making him imperfect and taking care of his enemy Water man's daughter.
Frankenstein reaches   HUMA lab and asks Shelly to make a pair for him so he can live normal life with love like a human need to live.

Shelly refuses his demand to do another crime…Frankenstein kidnapped Water girl from the lab.

Water man comes to know about Indira and reaches to meet her and his daughter.

Water man along with Indira reaches HUMA lab to see Water girl. Frankenstein destroyed everything in the lab, takes Water girl along and hides in the Alps… and demands to create a female Frankenstein for him, only then he will leave Water girl alive.

Water man reaches the Alps with the military force… they are searching for Water girl… Frankenstein appears and destroys all the force. William, Indira, Shelly with Ajay in the helicopter… Frankenstein attacks the helicopter and it falls down in the water. William with all the persons in it jumps out and hanged his head on the top of the tree.

Water man attacks Frankenstein… heavy fight between them.

Water man lost all his weapons during the fight… he made some sound to call all the animals… a group of white wolvew come to help Water man…Frankenstein disappears from there after seeing the animals, who were about to attack him.

Water man comes to help William and all… to land safly on the ground.

Frankenstein attacks him once more… Water man sees Water girl hanging on the top of the hill with the support of thin ice layer which could break any time.

Ice broke and Water girl started sliding down… on the top from the helicopter one hand (Ajay) comes out and saves Water girl.

Frankenstein attacks the helicopter and throws Ajay out of it… Water man comes in between and attacks Frankenstein.

While fighting, saving Water girl from Frankenstein, Shelly lost her life.

Water girl was saved and handed over to Indira.

Under water fight between Water man and Frankenstein… on the top of the water layer, Frankenstein's body comes out in so many pieces… Water man is inside the water… was he dead dead or alive... nobody knows.

WATERMAN

THE LEGEND OF EVOLUTION

SCREENPLAY

1994-INDIA

SCENE-A

LOCATION   : LAB UNDER GROUND -

DAY   : [INTERRIOR]

CHARACTERS   : BISHMACHARYA-SHELLY

Scene opens in a room…

Around 7 ft. tall… an incubator full of liquid…connected with lots of cables.

Camera moves forward close to the incubator…two green colored wings are moving and stopped. The wings are on the shoulders of a goat.

Electric spark near the incubator makes goat to stand and try to breath. Camera is panned to Shelly who is sitting near the computer giving shock treatment to the goat.

Computer displays the incubator on the screen…gets alert signal and break.

Cut to.

SCENE   -A1

LOCATION   : CABIN

DAY   : [INTERRIOR]

CHARACTERS : BISHMACHARYA-SHELLY

Dr. Acharya sitting in another cabin holding a book in his hand…he stands up with the sound of signal and book falls down from his hand.

Shelly enters in the frame.

They are very excited to see their experiment… is working.

Cut to

SCENE   -A2

LOCATION   : CABIN

DAY   : [INTERRIOR]

CHARACTERS   : BISHMACHARYA-SHELLY

The goat spreads its wings and tries to balance its body in the air. With the movement of shaft, the incubator falls down and breaks. Goat flies up and hits the top…falls down and tries to move again.

Shelly and Dr. Acharya enter and reach to the goat.

Cut to

SCENE A -3

LOCATION   : SCANNING DEPT.

DAY   : [INTERRIOR]

CHARACTERS : BISHMACHARYA-SHELLY-STAFF

In the scanning room, Shelly and Dr. Acharya enter with two ward boys holding the Goat in their hands. They tie it with the belt and start scanning.

The scanning screen shows the brain hammerage and weakness on shafts.

The reports of the scan make Shelly and Dr. Acharya more curious to experiment on it. Shelly finds that its wings are broken.

Cut to

SCENE A -4

LOCATION   : SCANNING DEPT.

DAY   : [INTERRIOR]

CHARACTERS : BISHMACHARYA- SHELLY -STAFF

Shelly and Dr. Acharya are with the student Ajay in the lab. Big screen display is showing the slide show of goat's body and wings parts.

Dr. Acharya: It's indeed a miracle! We have created life… that can survive on earth, air or water.   Even God never made any such creature. Now like an engineer we have to work on it. First we have to understand whole body mechanism than sketch the life we want to make. Shelly has done her anatomical engineering… now I give full authority to generate this flying creature (goat with wings).

Shelly gets emotional and tears of happiness start rolling down on her cheeks.
Shelly walks towards Dr. Acharya and he hands over a diary to her.

Dr. Acharya: This diary contains all the theories of the research in my life time. Now I am turning to my third revolution of human history called "FRANKENSTEIN".

Screen displays the skull of Frankenstein.
Camera moves 360 degrees to the skull.

Cut to.

SCENE A -5
LOCATION   : INCUBATOR LAB
DAY   : [INTERRIOR]
CHARACTERS : BISHMACHARYA -SHELLY-STAFF
                    FLYING HORSE- BUTTERFLY

In the cabin… which is made full of glass…. Shelly with her staff… making bandage to the flying animal (Goat). She gets a call from Dr. Acharya's cabin.

Shelly to staff: I will come back in sometime; do take care of it in my absence.

Shelly turns and moves towards Dr. Acharya's cabin.

Cut to
SCENE A -6
LOCATION   : DR. ACHARAYA'S CABIN
DAY   : [INTERRIOR]
CHARACTERS : BISHMACHARYA-SHELLY-STAFF
                    BUTTERFLY

Dr. Acharya's cabin…a big bucket full of flowers…honey is dripping down from them. A huge colorful butterfly is sitting on the flowers. A man is standing near the bucket *and Dr. Acharya is talking to the butterfly.*

Shelly enters in…Dr. Acharya turns to Shelly.

Dr Acharya: I have made the entire body of "Frankenstein". It is supported by steel rods and iron knee caps. This will support him to survive anywhere on this earth. Now we have to work on human parts.

Shelly is listening with all the excitement a person can have.

Cut to

SCENE A -7
LOCATION   : HUMAN SCULL ROOM.
DAY   : [INTERRIOR]
CHARACTERS : BISHMACHARYA- SHELLY

In the lab…few Red and Green cats are following colorful mice.

Dr. Acharya's voice over: Whole body is supported by steel rods and iron caps, it is moving with the motor and the Computer displays its total weight, which is 100.093 kg. and all is controlled by this remote.

Shelly moves near the body, it has no join between all the parts and it is covered with rubber fabric.

Cut to

SCENE A -8
LOCATION   : LAB.
DAY   : [INTERRIOR]
CHARACTERS : BISHMACHARYA- SHELLY-
                          STAFF -FRANKENSTEIN

A huge incubator…connected with lots of cables.
A man is lying inside in it and getting blood and other liquids through cables. In between very heavy electric sparks passing by.
On computer screen…camera is moving to his heart. Electric rays are making his heart ready to move.

Computer displays countdown…

Time: 64:84:00:00

Time left: 57:67:00:00

Time required: 72:00:00:00

Dr. Acharya *turns to* Shelly: You have to be patient at least for 720 hours (30 days)

Shelly: I am patient Dr. I have to be, I have waited for this all my life!

Dr. Acharya *keeps his hand on her shoulder & says*: Shelly, I was born to make Frankenstein but now I will say, WE ARE born to make Frankenstein. This is not mine alone, but ours.

Shelly: I know.

Cut to

SCENE A -9

LOCATION   : LAB.

NIGHT   : [EXTERIOR]

CHARACTERS : BISHMACHARYA-   SHELLY -FRANKENSTEIN

Outside, it is pouring heavily…there's thunder, light is sparking.

Frankenstein is lying in an incubator which is full of water. *An electric spark moves and fades in his toe. His finger starts moving.* His body is full of stitches. Right side of his face is covered with an iron helmet with camera in it, in the place of his eye.

One more thunder & electric spark makes his eyes open and start breathing; water bubble comes on the surface of the water tank.

He turns his face…a greenish thing (out of focus) comes towards the tank. He breaks the tank and water floods all over in the cabin.

Cut to

SCENE A -10

LOCATION   : LAB.

DAY   : [INTERRIOR]

CHARACTERS : BISHMACHARYA- SHELLY -FRANKENSTEIN

The goat spreads its wings and flies in the air.

Frankenstein screams and siren shows a red alert.

Camera on the shadow of the wall…shows *the fights between Frankenstein and goat… with heavy* sound effect. Blood spreads on the glass wall.

Cut to.

20 YEARS LATER

PARIS- 2014

SCENE 1

Location: Eiffel Tower Paris

Daytime : Exterior (Evening just before sunset)

Character: Old Indira.

The evening is foggy throughout (a cold misty evening), *the camera focuses on the poppy flowers which are arranged in a succession, the lawn is filled with greenery …..Now the camera focuses fully on the Eiffel Tower and the tall arena trees. The audio is very clear with the voice of the tourists, they are trying for an autograph* from the celebrity Indira –Indira is nearly forty yrs old; is wearing an Indian silk saree and her eyes are covered with specs. From the crowd, *Indira stands up and bids good-bye to her fans who have crowded near her.*

Cut to

Scene 1B

The camera captures the moving wheels of the Benz car, it stops and from the car… a handsome, tall man steps out, he is wearing a dark suit with hat on his head. He bears a cigar between his lips..exactly like Sherlock Holmes.

Cut to

Scene 1C

Character: Old Indira-William

Indira is sitting on a wooden chair behind the Eiffel and is reading the detective novel of Sherlock Holmes, *suddenly her mobile phone rings.* Indira closes the novel and attends the phone. She hears Williams' voice over the phone. (The phone call was from Williams).

Williams   reached in front of her and she disconnects the phone, Williams too disconnects it.

 Williams: I can spot out an Indian easily. *(Indira looks to herself dressed in saree)*

Williams : I know Sherlock Holmes too" *(Indira now looks into the cover-page of the novel she has in   her hand)*

Williams: All painters are fond of fiction and fantasy. They live in their dreams of fancy creations linked very much with their sadness and difficulties.

 Indira: I just finished reading this novel and you really resemble the character Sherlock Holmes. I feel that the character in this novel has come alive in front of me..I can't believe this!

Williams: Yes I have to be alive some how like Sherlock Holmes may be for you Indira.

(Indira smiles with a worried look in her face, anxious about why Williams has come to see her.)

    Indira: What can I do for you? Any inauguration of some Indian pavilion?

     Williams: See Indira, people need you for their entertainment & now you need   entertainment from somebody.

(Saying this Williams hands over the file kit and some discs.)

"See, you need to study and follow the instructions, if you believe".

(Indira opens the file.)

Cut to

Scene 2

Location: France Research Institute "xxxxx(HUMA),

Daytime : Exterior of the SIGNBOARD………..

Scene 3

Location: Huma Institute

Daytime ; Interior

Character: Shelly, Leher, Indira

Shelly's view.. to the entry of the Research centre… Shelly's both eyes centered towards the identification mirror and scanned with violet blurred lights……. *the steel door opens; there is a digital voice over the full body scan of Leher. They enter into the lift and it moves to the third underground floor (to the cellar).*

Cut to

Scene 4

Location: Huma Institute

Daytime ; Interior

Character: Shelly

Interior of the Huma Research Centre.

Shelly is the main character in this scene.

The camera takes us to a long corridor………..

The lift opens and the camera follows Shelly. She is passing through the different areas

in the building (the voice of electronic display).

She comes in front of a door and pauses there.

A voice calls out:

"Welcome Dr. Shelly"

she enters and the door closes by

itself from her back. There is a screen

in front of her. *Dr Shelly's details come to the screen.*

Cut to...

Scene 5
Location: Huge Aquarium
Daytime ; Interior
Characters: Shelly, Leher, Indira

The camera focuses behind the glass water tank. *The door opens and a lady enters wearing a saree (it is Indira).* The camera does not show Indira clearly. *The camera now takes a turn into the water;* two eyes are visible in the water-a *quick shot back to Indira* (still not clear of the images due to the water flow and faded lights). The background has a light music which is audible. In the faded light there is a brightened glow in the water, and the uplift view of the fish structured mermaid is visible. *Now the camera clears the image of Indira,* Indira is worried and doubtful about the creature in the water tank.

Cut to

Scene 6
Location: Huge Aquarium
Daytime ; Interior
Characters: Shelly, Leher, Indira

The camera now focuses on the mermaid typing something on the keyboard and the digital audio says" Welcome to the most beloved mother"...............
Welcome to the most beloved mother"-it was the voice
of Shelly *and she enters in.* Worried Indira is now relaxed after seeing Shelly. Shelly and Indira have started conversations:

Shelly: You are going to meet your daughter.

Shelly continues: Indira you are going to see a miracle". The amazing Miracle made by you!!" (Indira still confused). *Shelly presses the remote button – the huge glass door opens with a built up music.....and there lies the mermaid (watergirl- Leher)... comes to the screen...swimming in the water.*

Indira's unbelievable reaction ………wants to feel her, wants to talk to her daughter. Leher feels the same & Leher wants to speak to her mother… both very emotional………… unable to speak……*Indira touches the glass in the hope of touching Leher….. Leher too does the same. Out of the emotions Leher's glands starts reacting and she starts glowing-* Glowing brighter and brighter…… *Shelly immediately takes Indira out of the hall.*

Cut to

Scene 7
Location: Shelly's cabin
Night time: Interior
Characters: Shelly, Leher, Indira

Shelly is listening to the internal minds of Indira. Indira is slowly returning back to her memory. The camera is bringing flash backs back to Indira's memory…..the flash back memories of the mermaid.   Indira yells and stands up…… she shouts "She can't be my daughter! I don't have one……..I was alone and a spinster for the last 20yrs….   "Are you fooling me? I can't believe….. Who are you? Where am I? Why have you taken me here? Tell me who was that………. What was that? It was not a human figure! How can I give birth to a dragon of this kind?"…….Shelly is silent..unable to reply. *Indira loses consciousness & falls o the floor.*

 Cut to

Scene 8
Location: Research Center
Day time: Exterior
Characters: Shelly- Indira

Indira and Shelly are discussing….*There voices dissolve and mix with the electronic sound.*
Camera pulls back and travels 200 km with the sound, travels from the Institute to the forest and reaches to the mountain of Iceberg to a cave where it gets blasted at 2000 power volt.
(This was the power of Frankenstein who heard them talking.)

Cut to

Scene 9
Location: Water girl's Aquarium
Night time: Interior
Characters: Water girl-Shelly- Staff

Water girl is lying in the water pond & can barely breathe… is struggling to have sufficient oxygen. *Dr. Shelly comes in the room with 2 senior Doctors to examine her. They treat her (water girl) with specially added Oxi- water… direct to her mouth.*
Water girl is not able to swallow the water and vomits her lungs out containing some blood. Her gills throw out the bubble of water and blood, she gets exhausted and falls under the water level and comes up with the water bounce. A Scan unit is fixed on her body to examine all organs movements. Dr. makes her wear a mask to open her mouth and fixes a camera to see through her throat.

Cut to

Scene 10
Location: Water girl's Aquarium
Night time: Interior
Characters: Water girl-Shelly-Senior Dr.-Staff

On the scan of the monitor, watergirl's inner throat is shown. *The Video graph is moving which shows the big size bubbles continues   moving and not gets blasted.*
Shelly rewinds it and replays it. After seeing the continues .process of the bubble she starts getting worried. *Senior Dr. comes in and starts explaining her* about the scan bubble which is a throat tumor and can has to be cured by an operation.

Cut to

Scene 11
Location: Special Ward
Night time: Interior
Characters: Indira-Shelly-Nurse

In casualty (pin drop silence)... Indira seems very perplexed. She is lying on the bed, her hand is on saline with glucose travelling to her body through the saline pipe.

Shelly enters the room and takes Indira to see water girl. Shelly explains the entire scanned report about water girl's tumor and that it can be cured by an immediate operation. While listening to all, Indira gets emotional and somewhere in her

heart   she gets convinced to be water girl's mother.

Cut to.

Scene 12

Location: Water girl cabin

Night time: Interior

Characters: Water girl- Indira-Shelly-Crew

Water girl is getting treated by the crew of doctors working under Dr. Shelly. Indira enters the room with an emotional smile on her face. Water girl sees Indira and for the first time she feels the tears that are rolling down on her cheeks. The tears drip and dissolve in water, slowly her fingers start moving towards the keyboard as she wants to say something.

With her fingers moving, first thing she writes "MA". Indira gets the flashbacks of her young life which practically does not exist according to her; but some thing is forcing her to believe it all. Shelly notices Indira is going through something which is troubling her and asks her to spend some time alone with water girl before they take her to the operation theatre. Indira walks near watergirl, with the motherhood ex-precision on her face.

    Shelly: I am her mother too, I brought her up for last 20 years.

Water girl murmurs   the word "ma".

After hearing "Ma" Shelly's eyes got wet and tear starts rolling down.

  Shelly: I was her only mother till now but I am happy that she got her real mother who gave her birth.

Water girl: (Digital Voice Over) Mother when can I see

my father?

Indira and Shelly exchange the look and turned to Water girl.

Shelly made the key of digital sound signal to answer her question.

  Indira: (Murmurs) My daughter, can't speak, can't even

hear us.

Shelly: (To Indira) She can understand the feelings and make

        conversation through magnetic digital sound signal. Which we

      have made only for her.

Shelly points out the cabin opposite Water girls room, from they can make   conversation with Watergirl .

       Cut to

Scene 13

Location: Micro phone cabin

Night time: Interior

Characters: Water girl- Indira-Shelly-Crew

Water girl is lying in the water tank and taking external oxygen from her mouth and nose, like humans do. *All of sudden, she starts moving and searching; her eyes get stuck on the opposite cabin, from where her mother (Indira) is trying to talk with her.*

    Indira: (with heavy throat) Daughter I have not been

with you all those years when you need the most to be with your mother.(sobbing) please forgive me for this. My daughter, now I will be always with you.

(Shelly is also listening through head phone)

Water girl's lips start moving and she tries to make a conversation with her mother. She tries to lift up her body but unable to do so. Bubbles are coming out of her ears. Indira is eagerly waiting for her daughter to speak. Suddenly, she realizes that her daughter cannot speak and stretches her lips with a heartbroken smile.

 Indira: My child, I missed all the moments of your childhood. I wish your father would have been here. He was very good human, not a human, he was as good as God is. He did a lot for humanity, which God only can do. He had some extraordinary miraculous powers which a normal human can't have. He always lived in water or in caves."

 Indira looks up and says, "He sees you from Heaven and I m sure u must be very happy. Nobody saw him in day time, the whole world was against him and they thought he was a dragon. But I know, for me he was the eleventh birth of Lord Vishnu. And you are the shadow of your father."
Shelly is listening to this all.

Water girl is curiously listening about her father.

Indira goes in the flashback and thinks all the things which Waterman done for the sake of people.

Flash back: Many army people came to kill Waterman. They are bombing in the water.
Suddenly the mike falls down from Indira's hand.
Due to which, Water girl gets some signal problem and turns her look to her mother. Door opens and the senior doctor enters in and ask for 20 minutes to re-scan Watergirl.
After re-scanning, he goes in other room and sees the report on scan computer, tumor has almost gone.
Shelly is filled with surprise.
Indira is filled with joy and comes out to hug her daughter.

Cut to

Scene 14
Location: Huma Lab
Night time: Interior
Characters: Senior Dr. - Shelly-Crew

Shelly with the senior Dr. and staff are watching on scanning monitor. Water girl's tumor has become worst than ever, is on the edge of bursting.
They are all in tension, waiting for the worst to happen. Pin drop silence… suddenly her tumor blasts and water girl who was on the surface of the water slowly gets drowned.
Shelly's reaction is as if she lost her daughter.

Cut to

Scene 15

Location: Water girl Tank

Night time: Interior

Characters: Water girl

Water girl is lying under the water, like other water species. She gets the signal that something is trying to reach up to her. *With a split of second, water girl opens her eyes turns her face to the direction from where the signal is coming.*

Cut to

Scene 16

Location: Micro phone cabin

Night time: Interior

Characters: Water girl- Indira-Shelly-Crew

In the scanning room, Shelly is sitting in the pain of losing her daughter.. all the doctors are also in pain.. feeling that they lost their patient. All of sudden, a green signal comes on the monitor and its starts showing that Water girl is coming back and her blasted tumor is getting cured. They are extremely shocked, look at each other as if some miracle is happening which is not possible in medical science but they have to believe it. Finally, miracle happens and her tumor gets cured.

Cut to

Scene 17

Location: Micro phone cabin

Night time: Interior

Characters: Water girl- Indira-Shelly-Crew

Behind Water girl's tank...a shadow is moving, Water girl turns her face and nothing is there. Then behind the glass door, some finger is moving and leaves the finger print on the door.

Cut to

Scene 18

Location: Indira's bedroom

Night time: Interior

Characters: Indira

Indira gets up from her sleep, like she has had a nightmare and gets the intuition that something wrong is going to happen with water girl.

Cut to

FLASH BACK STORY ABOUT WATER MAN BEFORE 20 YEARS (IN INDIA)

Scene 19

Location: College of Fine Arts

Day time: Interior-Studio(Painting)

Characters: Indira-Manasi-Professor-Manish

In the class room… professor and Manasi (Indira's friend) react on something.

Indira: (voice over) I had this dream for many days; I have named it as "Waterman". Professor: I know this can be only your imagination… not real.

Manasi: Sir, she has been saying that he exists somewhere.

Professor: I know all of your work comes from your imagination.

That's why it's so original and unique. You have got the Lalit Kala award for your last work, "The Pardon", so now I am more curious to know about your dream.

Manasi: Sir, she always told me about her 'waterman' dream but I never thought this way. She has been living with that man in her dreams. Sometimes I think its   madness to live with a dream.

Professor: If you will read history, you will find that all the great painters, sculptors and even poets live with their dreams and in that they have different emotions…

In the 15th century,   Leonardo-da Vinci had a dream about the motion to be captured by camera. He drew his imagination on canvas…and here we are…today everybody knows about the motion camera, so his dream was the pioneer of the motion camera.

He turns to Indira, "I can see that you have very bright future."

Cut to

Scene 20

Location: College of Fine Arts

Daytime: Interior-Studio(Painting)

Characters: Indira-Manasi-Professor-Manish

[as it is like our hero WATER MAN]
DESOLVE with the waves.

Cut to
Scene 21

Location: Sea

Day time: Exterior

Characters: Indira-Manasi-Professor-Manish-Guide

YEAR AD-1996 SOUTH AFRICA.

Wide shot…far from the sea, smoke is coming up and touching the sky…whole sky is covered with smoke.

Guide voice over: Behind the sea, you can see smoke coming.. that's the Volcano…nobody has lived here for the last 25 years; people are scared to come here; because it can blast any time.

1976 was the last time it erupted and ruined every human being, every tree, even all species around the sea.

One more natural disaster is "Tornado".

When volcano gets more powerful, it leaves the waste under the water, which creates the tornado.

So, its essential that we cross this as early as possible to reach island as it is too dangerous to be here for long time.

Indira's reaction, after listening to all of it…she starts thinking about her dream, same location. (Steady cam shots- flash cuts)

She is seeing all the things just like it is in her recurrent dream.

Thunder, lightening…clouds become more darker…only thing which they can see is the volcano burning.

All the students start singing and dancing in the boat…professor also enjoys this.

Indira is lost in her dreams.

Indira's boyfriend (Manish) comes closer and holds her hand to dance but she refuses and is still lost in her dreams.

Far away, a huge wave of water is coming towards her followed by another…she screams out her lungs…every wave is joining the another and is transforming into a kind of big pillar(like a Tsunami). All the other students are unable to hear her screaming.

There's thunder and lightning…light falls down in the tsunami and produces multicolors in water.

All the students also see it and stop dancing, professor switches off the music… now the boat is losing its balance and tornado is travelling towards them. All of them hold each other and shout for help. Some of them fall down in the water, Indira falls on the other side of the boat and finally boat sinks in.

Cut to

Scene 22

Location: Crab Island

Day time: Exterior

Characters: Indira-Manasi-Professor-Manish

Scene opens…in a very beautiful small island…sunrise…early in the morning. Indira is lying near a rock…slowly…she opens her eyes.

Some of the students are freezing…few of them are missing. Manish is helping another student to come out from the sea.

Professor is trying the mobile to call someone for help but the network is dead. Manish finds Manasi's body in the water…Indira starts crying when she sees that Manasi is dead.

Cut to

Scene 23

Location: Hostel

Night time: Interior

Characters: Indira-Manasi

Flashes about Manasi:

In the hostel room…Indira is making a painting…Manasi comes in and disturbs her…runs out…Indira is following her.

Manasi makes Indira laugh.

Cut to

Scene 24

Location: Crab Island

Day time: Exterior

Characters: Indira-Manasi-Professor-Manish

Indira is smiling … with nostalgia on her face.

Suddenly she realises…Manasi is dead.(reaction)

Indira: Because of you, we planned the world tour and you only left me in

between…God is really cruel with us.

She gets up and runs behind a big rock…starts crying.

Cut to

Return from the flash back (AD 2014)

Scene 25

Location: Huma Lab

Night time: Interior

Characters: Indira-water girl- Shelly

Indira is in the cabin…opposite the microphone, crying….

Water girl speaks for the first time" Ma"(audio transition).

Indira's reaction…

Shelly's reaction…

Water girl is curious to know more about her father.

Indira goes to her daughter…feels her finger…face…and gives her something to eat.

Shelly Interrupts: Tell us more about…What happened after that? How and where had you met "Waterman"?

Cut to

Scene 26

Location: Crab Island

Day time: Exterior

Characters: Indira

FALASH BACK CONTINUES (YEAR-1976)

INDIRA touches the part of a special stone carved by humans with their hands[hand connection from scene:55 Water girl's hand]

and feel the finishing of the stone. She finds some hindi letters on the carvings with the names DEV and NATHALIA.

A sign of arrow indicates the entrance of the cave.

Indira moves ahead.

Waves come in and fill half the level of the cave. She falls in to the water and rolls down inside the cave.

Cut to

Scene 27

Location: Cave

Day time: Interior (low Light)

Characters: Indira

Indira opens her eyes and screams out her lungs. She is seeing her dream with open eyes, which is real & true!

Her reaction from different-different angles.

Cut to

flashes about the dreams

Scene 28

Location: Cave

Day time: Interior (low Light)

Characters: Indira

Steady cam shots of the cave. (EFX)

Indira realizes it was not the dream but reality. All over the cave spider nets…fungus. She finds some thick liquid under her eye…rotates her eye ball but unable to find…finally she touches, it was blood which came out when she fell. She screams…(echo sound effect). She is scared…wants to run away from there. All over its slippery, unable to stand even. Some light passes by her inside the cave…she starts following the lights. Birds flew on the top of her head.

Cut to

Scene 29

Location: Rock Sculpture

Day time: Exterior

Characters: Indira

Indira gets surprised after sees something…(reaction 360 degree round trolley)

She closes her eyes…opens them…still in surprise…removes the water from her face. She looks around…a blurred (out of focus) huge image.

Image gets covered with a huge wave of water, she gets curious and wants to see it again, wave comes forward and splashes on the face.

Water in the air…comes down in slow motion (her close up)

(trolley movement- EFX).

Cut to.

Scene 30

Location: Rock Sculpture

Day time: Exterior

Characters: Water man Indira

Wide shot…heavy wave returns back to the huge rock (which looks like a human sculpture) and splashes to spread in the air…water goes in and comes out from the eyes and the mouth of the sculpture…water drips down from the hair … it produces the bubble in the water.

(This is the way which is made by small rocks to reach to the sculpture.)

She runs and jumps from one rock to another to find the cave which is on the bottom of the rock.

The closer she reaches, more curious she gets to see its inner part.

She stops in front of the sculpture…looks from top to bottom…

The sculpture is in the shape of a female head. It has a silver chain in its neck with a blue stone.

The rock (which faces sunset) is full of some carving which is in Hindi and English and she can barely read because water is continuously hitting it.

She comes down from the cave…its evening, everything is looking golden and beautiful… sun is setting down…she realizes that she has lost her friends group and turns to move from there.

She turns…and the chain with blue stone falls in her neck.

She touches it…holds it and sees it.

Flash back: her dream Water man is making her wear the same chain.

Cut to…

Scene 31
Location: Sea Shore
Evening: Exterior (Sun Set)
Characters: Manish- Friends

Scene opens on the Island …two boats are standing on the shore…Army people are loading dead
bodies in one boat and some students are getting inside the same boat.
Few are eating food…given by naval food supply…one boat goes away.
Another boat is just ready to move…Manish starts looking for Indira(he is tired)
 Professor: Indira is not here, she must be in another boat.
Manish didn't want to take any risk…starts searching all over.
        Friend: She is not here I have already searched her all over this place.

    Manish: O.k. let's go and catch the first boat…as fast as possible.

Cut to

Scene 32
Location: Crab Island (Sun Set)
Evening: Exterior
Characters: Indira

INDIRA reaches on the shore of island… nobody is there.
She is screaming and calling everyone by their names…gets tired and sits on the sand. She sees the
chain she was holding in her hand, then looks up to the sky. Birds fly away… Clouds are heavy and
dark …then thunder starts,
(Special sound effect) makes her scared.
She stands up and sees a very big whale is coming towards her like a huge ship.
She takes her feet backwards. It comes closer & closer.
Somebody is sitting on it and riding it!

She turns to run from there…turns back…the whale is singing in the water…and an image is standing to her right side.

Indira keeps quite and slowly turns.

 Camera is on Water man's feet…violet color liquid is falling from top to bottom. His legs are strange, not like human but like a duck…all fingers are joined.

Indira moves aback and looks at his face.

Water man is standing in front of her…looks green and silver with red patches. Ears are moving and some liquid is dripping down from his ear's gill.

Indira's dream Flash cuts.

 Water man gets scared and disappears in the water.

 Indira gets unconscious and falls down.

Cut to

Scene 33

Location: Human Island

Nighttime: Exterior

Characters: Water man- Indira

Water man comes out of the water and sees her.

She is lying unconscious on the shore.

Water man reaches near her and tries to touch her but he is scared to do that.

Water man comes closer and looks around, nobody is there. He sees the chain she is still holding in her hand.

He sits near her and touches her hand. It's the first time after his mother and father died, he has touched a human body!

Touch of a human gave him a jolt which he had never felt before. He moves his hand and gets curious to touch her again.

He watches her whole body from top to bottom, he sees her lips, breasts, eyes …and than sees himself…he feels something different and strange.

Once again, he touches her face.

Indira's eyes are closed but start moving inside as she is getting conscious.

Water man takes the chain from her hand and jumps in the water.

Indira is silently watching him.

From far, Water man thanks her (by action) for giving his treasure back.

Cut to

Scene 34

Location: Sea Shore

Night time: Exterior

Characters: Water man- Indira

Water man jumps in the water…starts swimming and goes deep in the sea. While breathing, bubbles are coming out on the surface of the water.

Cut to

Scene 35

Location: Sea shore

Night time: Exterior

Characters: Water man- Indira

Water man comes out of the water, reaches the shore… where Indira is lying unconscious.

Waterman is worried … she is covered with snow.

Water man comes and sits near her… he holds her in his hand and stands up to move. .

Cut to

Scene 36

Location: Human Scull Rock cave

Night time: Interior

Characters: Water man- Indira

He jumps in the water holding her and reaches for the way to the cave. He jumps faster & faster from one stone to another.

He puts her down near his cave, makes some fire near the cave and sits besides her. He looks very sad to see her unconscious.

Cut to

Scene 37
Location: Human Scull Rock cave
Morning: Interior
Characters: Water man- Indira

Sun rises behind the sculpture cave. Indira opens her eyelids and sees two skulls beside her. She gets scared…stands up to move away.
Something attracts her mind…she stops.

Cut to

Scene 38
Location: Sea Shore
Morning: Exterior
Characters: Water man

Water man is reaching to the shore…screaming as he is talks to birds that are flying up in the sky!
He returns back to Indira…carrying some flowers and fruits in his hands.

Cut to

Scene 39
Location: Rock
Day: Exterior
Characters: Water man- Indira

Waterman comes near Indira, puts all the flowers and fruits near her and jumps back into the sea.

Indira tries to speak to him but before she can say something he disappears. She tries to search for him in the water.

 Cut to

Scene 40

Location: Micro phone cabin

Night time: Interior

Characters: Water girl- Indira-Shelly

Present….

In the room, three of them…a silent pause for 5 seconds, Water girl is silent and sad. She looks just like his father. Now they are more curious to know the story ahead.

Indira: I was so scared of him but at the same time I wanted him to be around. He never spoke to me or he dint know how to speak. He just always made some unnatural sounds which I could not understand. There was no one I could talk to. This was making me go crazy.
I lost my family, my friends… I thought Manish would come back for me but nobody came.
So one day I tried to escape from there, I saw a boat in the middle of the sea, jumped in the sea and tried to reach to the boat.
Shelly and Water girl are silently listening to her and looking at her face.

Cut to

Scene 41

Location: Crab island (Middle of the Sea)

Day: Exterior

Characters: Water man- Indira

Indira is swimming towards the boat, she screams to grab attention but the boat is too far from her so noone is able to hear her. She gets very tired and collapses in.

Cut to

Scene 42

Location: Crab island (Middle of the Sea)

Day: Exterior

Characters: Water man- Indira

Camera is behind Indira (her suggestion).

Boat reaches the shore…Manish comes out of the boat with the navy staff and starts looking for Indira…(calling her name with a loudspeaker) They search the entire island.

Cut to

Scene 43

Location: Cave

Day time: Interior (low Light)

Characters: Indira

Water man is in his cave…hears the sound which is very strange to him.

He goes under the water and reaches towards the propeller of the ship, which is moving very fast with a very heavy sound.

Cut to

Scene 44

Location: Crab Island (Middle of the Sea)

Day: Exterior

Characters: Water man- Whale

Scene opens under the water…boat moves.

After searching for Indira for a long time…all of them go to the boat and start to go back.

Boat picks up its speed.

Water man is sitting on a whale…followed by 10 whales… which looks like big ship itself … is following the boat, reaches near and boat turns and all of them fall in the water and die.

Cut to

Scene 45

Location: Crab Island (Under Water)

Day: Exterior

Characters: Water man- Indira- Whales

Indira is moving under the water (Slow motion) tired, out of breath.

She is surrounded by fishes.

Water man enters in the frame…he is riding on a whale.

He takes her on his shoulders and move towards the cave.(EFX)

Cut to

Scene 46

Location: Crab Island (Under Water)

Day: Exterior

Characters: Water man- Indira- Whales

Far…boat is sinking down…and fading out.

Water man comes out of water…Indira is lying unconscious on his shoulders.

Her stomach is full of water…eyes are closed…barely breathing.

Water man gets panicked to see this…doesn't know what to do.

Cut to

Scene 47

Location: Crab Island (Under Water)

Day: Exterior

Characters: Water man-Whales

Flash back.

A dolphin is unable to breathe…mud and fungus is stuck in it.

Water man holds the dolphin by its tail and turns it up side down…all the fungus and mud comes out
from its mouth…

Cut to

Scene 48
Location: Sea Shore
Day: Exterior
Characters: Water man- Indira- Whales

Water man lifts up Indira by her legs, turns her upside down and shakes her.
All the water comes out…she starts coughing.

She opens her eyes…(her head is down and legs are up)and sees everything upside down… the way it was before.
She sees water and Water man's legs.

Water man makes her sit in the water and runs away.
Indira is still breathing hard…she calls Waterman.
Indira: Water man please come and take me to my land…
She starts crying.

After seeing Indira crying, he gets violet color liquid in his eyes. (he is crying)

Indira stops crying and starts staring at him.
They both are looking at each other. (round trolley 360 degree)
Cut to…

Scene 49
Location: Sea Shore
Morning: Exterior
Characters: Water man- Indira

Early morning sunrise… Camera travels inside the cave…Water man opens his eyes and starts looking for Indira…she is not there. He searches around but can't find her. He comes out of the cave …her clothes are lying on the top of a big stone.

He moves ahead …Indira is behind the rock…she peeps out from the back of the rock and asks him to stop right there.

Water man throws her dress towards her; she wears it and comes out.

Cut to.

Scene 50

Location: Cave

Day: Interior

Characters: Water man- Indira

Water man enters the cave with Indira …

Waterman lifts up a rock behind the skulls. It is too dark, some flies come out and jump inside the seller, he asks her to come inside but she is scared to go inside, Waterman holds her to make her comfortable so she can come down. They are standing opposite to each other… hugging each other.

Camera round trolley…Staring at each other.

Water man realizes and puts her down, removes his hand from her waist.

Water man opens another rock…inside; there are so many skulls of sea animals and so many different kind of shells.

He offers her one of his treasures which is his mothers dress, she accepts and says thanks to him.

Cut to

Scene 51

Location: Sea Shore

Morning: Exterior

Characters: Water man- Indira

Water man is coming towards the cave…holding some fruits in his hands and is accompanied by adolphin.

He goes inside the cave…searches for Indira…she is not there.

He sees her footsteps…follows them.

Indira is in a tribal dress…feeling shy to come in front of Water man.

Water man is staring at her.. from top to bottom, than he looks at himself.

He moves ahead to touch her.

She takes a step back and run towards the sea.

Cut to

Scene 52

Location: Sea Shore

Morning: Exterior

Characters: Water man- Indira

Indira is sitting on the rock…right opposite the cave…thinking and smiling.

Water man is watching her from a distance. Suddenly she starts crying.

Camera is on her face…one hand enters and wipes the tears from her cheeks.

Water man holding some fruits in other hand…offers those fruits to her to eat. She takes those and starts eating…some liquid from the fruit comes out and falls in her eyes. Within a fraction of second…she closes her eyes and starts screaming with pain…

Water man holds the air in his mouth and blows it in her eyes…she feels better.

Their eyes and lips are close to each other…accidently their lips touch each other. She gets embarrassed, stands, he also stands with her.

They look at each other…slowly she hugs him.

For the first time, he feels the touch of a female.

[360 degree moves.]

Cut to

Scene 53

Location: Middle of the Sea

Day: Exterior

Characters: Water man- Indira-Whales

Water man is in the water with a group of dolphins…He is riding on a dolphin and Indira is sitting behind him. Other dolphins are following them, they go under the water. It's an amazing experience for Indira, which she experiences   for the first time…

She is screaming…after some time…she can't breathe properly…so they come out of the water.

Cut to

Scene 54

Location: Island (Near Volcano)

Evening: Exterior

Characters: Water man- Indira- Whales)

Water man and Indira are on the other sea shore …Indira is laughing and tears are coming out of her eyes.

She gets tired and breathes heavily.

Water man stands near her, arches his body… he makes some sound and thousands of birds flow away in one time from there. He spits some blood with a blue liquid.

Indira gets up….

Indira : Why does this blue liquid come out of your mouth when you get tired? What

 is this?

Water man looks at her and smiles, then he turns his face and waves to dolphins…that are going back to sea.

Indira: What is this..the volcano?

Water man doesn't reply but raises his finger towards the cave, which is far from them (out of focus).

Sun is setting down…everything is looking beautiful around.

They start swimming together towards the cave.

Cut to

Scene 55
Location: Island (Near Volcano)
Night: Exterior
Characters: Water man- Indira

While swimming…something falls in front of them with a very heavy sound effect. It is very bright.
Water man looks back…volcano is blasting…and a very heavy fire ball is coming towards them.
He takes Indira along and goes deep in the water.
Fire ball makes the water reddish and it starts boiling.

Cut to

Scene 56
Location: Cave
Evening: Interior
Characters: Water man- Indira

Water man opens the window of the cave.
Around it, many black stones are lying because of the eruption of the volcano… far from cave he sees the dead body of one of his dolphin friends.
Water man holds Indira's hand and comes out from cave.

Cut to

Scene 57

Location: Rock

Day: Exterior

Characters: Water man- Indira- Whales)

They climb up on the rock…
Water man shows her the carving and asks her to read it.

Cut to

Scene 58

Location: Rock

Day: Exterior

Characters: Water man- Indira

Camera on the text… half of the text is covered with mud…a heavy wave splashes on the text and takes all the mud along.

Indira starts reading aloud: My name is Dharamputra, I was a Lawyer. When I heard about African freedom fighter Nelson Mandela, I got so fascinated that I left my practice and started writing about their freedom. Considering that it might help them to tell their thoughts to the public. With the help of a dear friend of mine, Halidou Sali famous poet from Bibemi, we started our journey to Volcano Island.

Text dissolves with the flashback scenes..

Cut to.

Scene 59

Location: Middle of the sea

Day: Exterior

Characters: Dharam Putra- Halidou Sali

Year -1944.

Camera is under the water…sun's rays are falling on top of the water…*boat enters in the frame.*
Storm in the water… *two of them in the boat, struggling to reach to the sea shore.*
Very heavy wave comes in front of the camera.

Camera on the top… heavy force of the wave… *boat stands straight in the air…Dharamaputra falls down in the sea.*

Boat turns down and Halidou Sali falls and is thrown on a rock. His head breaks in two parts.

Cut to.

Scene 60
Location: Rock
Early Morning: Exterior
Characters: Dharam Putra- Halidou Sali

Dharamputra is extremely tired… *is holding onto a rock…and lying in the water. With slight consciousness, he sits on the rock…*

Camera rotates around 360 degree…its foggy, misty and unfocused. Far from him… volcano is burning.

Camera rotates and dissolve to text..

Cut to.

Scene 61
Location: Rock
Day: Exterior
Characters: Water man- Indira

Water man enters with Indira in the frame and takes her to another part of the rock so as to read the remaining carvings.

Indira starts reading the text.

Voice over: I stayed six months in the middle of the sea. In summer, the water went off (level went down). I tried to find an island around, nothing was there but water. I came back and started living on this rock.

Cut to.

Scene 62

Location: Rock

Day: Exterior

Characters: Dharam Putra

Flash back conti…

Wide shot…*camera is moving towards Dharamputra…within a split of second camera turns…he is stabbing a fish with a stone…*
Fish breaks apart…
His hand reaches to the water…suddenly he notices that the water level is down. Waterman jumps in the water washes the fish and eats it…fade out….

Cut to…

Scene 63

Location: Rock

Evening: Exterior

Characters: Dharam Putra

Dharamputra is swimming in the water…holding a fish in his mouth. He reaches to the rock.
Rock is bigger than ever…(his reaction). *He climbs up the rock and sits. He takes a sharp stone and starts carving on the rock…so as to write his Autobiography.*

Cut to…

Scene 64
Location: Rock
Day: Exterior
Characters: Dharam Putra- Natalya- Men

Fade in …Dharamputra's beard is grown up…he is lying on the rock.
He sees so many bodies are lying in the water. He jumps in the water and takes a body along… he sees
that it (he) has no life. Dharamputra take the dead body's clothes off… ties with a big stone and drowns it
in the water.
He does the same with 2nd dead body.

When he takes third body in his hand…it starts moving.
She is a European girl. He turns her body and all the water in her stomach comes out.
She starts breathing heavily.

Cut to.

Scene 65
Location: Rock
Evening: Exterior
Characters: Dharam Putra- Natalya

Dharamputra sitting is on the rock with girl (Natalya), talking and eating the fish.

Natalya : Why didn't you escape from here?
  Dharamputra: I tried…but you have to have a boat or something
which can take you away from here. This place is too far from any island. So many dangerous sharks
and other species are here which will not let you cross the sea.

Fade out…

Cut to.

Scene 66

Location: Rock

Day: Exterior

Characters: Dharam Putra- Natalya

Six months later.

Water level has come up…little part of the rock is visible.
They are sitting on the rock… *a heavy wave comes and goes from the top of their head.*
It's becoming more & more difficult to breathe.
They stand up on the rock…water level comes up more high up to Dharam Putra's head level.
Water level has crossed Natalya's head…he lifts her up out of water in his hands and stays like that…whole night.
Like this many days pass.

Cut to.

Scene 67

Location: Rock

Day: Exterior

Characters: Dharam Putra- Natalya-Small boy

We converted this rock into a cave and made this place possible to live in.
We lived in here like this for 20 years. Many times, Natalya got pregnant but because of the climate…we lost our child.

20 years later...

Dharamputra and Natalya get old.
Natalya is nine months pregnant…she delivers a boy.
They are taking care of him. (flash cuts)
He is one year old…playing with small fishes around him…riding on a big shark. (flash cuts)

Cut to.

Scene 68

Location: Rock

Evening: Exterior

Characters: Dharam Putra- Natalya-Small boy

Natalya dies… and leaves her one year old son behind.

After 5 years.

Dharma putra dies…and leaves his 6 years old son alone.

Fade out and dissolve to the text…

Cut to.

Scene 69

Location: Rock

Day: Exterior

Characters: Water man- Indira

Indira has finished reading and looks at Water man.
Waterman holds her hand and takes her inside the cave…
He removes a stone…and both of them go underground in the cave, where he has his father and mother's skulls.
Water man speaks for the first time… "MOTHER" and "FATHER"

Indira's reaction…that he can speak.

She starts teaching him…(flash cuts)

6 Months later

Water man and Indira talking…

Indira picks up a fruit in her hand and asks him…

Indira : What is this called?

Water man: (smiles) This is an Orange…don't teach me…I know everything and can speak very well..

Indira: (shocked) to see him speaking very fluently.

They both burst into laughing… enjoying the very moment.

Cut to.

Scene 70

Location: Sea

Day: Exterior

Characters: Water man- Indira-Whales

Water man: Indira come with me…I will take you a place you have never seen.

A whale comes and starts playing in the water…

It comes up and goes deep down in the water, Water man sits on and takes Indira along. Water man starts riding on it.

Cut to.

Scene 71

Location: Sea

Day: Exterior

Characters: Water man- Indira-Whales

Camera is far…

Water man is riding the whale towards the camera. Indira is sitting behind.

Their close reaction… Indira is happy ..feels like she is in Seventh Heaven… for her it's an impossible dream that she is living!

They reach closer to the camera…something very bright red in color (out of focus) falls…in slow motion, in front of them.

A very huge tower in front of them.

They look up…it's the volcano…which is throwing fire in the water.

Everything around looks so beautiful. Their love is blooming with nature.

Water man: Close your eyes, take a deep breath and hold it.

They go deep in the water.

   Water man: now open your eyes..

They are deep in the water…colorful fishes around them…Indira's hair is flying in the water in slow motion…water bubbles are coming out…tiny plants…sea sells around them. Water man explains everything in the sea around.

Indira is out of breath and asks him to come out…

They come out …Indira is out of breath…

Indira breathes heavily…her eyes are red because of salt water.

Water man sees and laughs…Indira gives an expression of anger mixed with love.

Cut to.

Scene 72

Location: Sea

Day: Exterior

Characters: Few Men-boat

(Out of focus) A water boat is coming from far… towards Water man's cave.

Scene 73

Location: Sea

Day: Exterior

Characters: Water man- Indira-Whales

Indira hears a sound of a water boat.

Before Indira can say anything, Water man again goes inside the water.

Cut to.

Scene 74

Location: Cave

Day: Exterior

Characters: Indira

Cave is in the frame…

Indira enters in the frame… tired…breathing heavily…

Indira searches for the boat around but nothing is there.

She sees a few footprints on the soil and follows those.

Following the foot prints, she reaches inside the cave…the foot prints disappear.

She hears water boat sound…

She turns and runs outside the cave by the time she reaches out, water boat is far…

Indira calls Water man and asks him to take her to the boat.

Cut to

Scene 75

Location: Sea

Day: Exterior

Characters: Water man- Indira-Whales

Water man and Indira are following the boat.

Cut to

Scene 76

Location: Sea

Day: Exterior

Characters: Water man- Indira-Whales-Few Men

Boat is running too fast…. two men are sitting in it.

With a jump in the air, Water man enters in the boat…with Indira.
Gunshots…these 2 men start firing. Water man gets hurt and falls into the water.
Men are still firing all over in the water.
    Indira: (shouting) Please stop firing…we need your help.
Camera on the top… Water man grabs the boat from behind.
Water man comes in the boat…

Fight between them.   (fast cuts)
Men fall into the sea.

Cut to.

Scene 77

Location: Sea

Day: Exterior

Characters: Water man- Indira-Whales

    Indira: We should turn the boat and save those men.
They must have thought we want to kill them, that's why they fired on us.

Water man turns the boat… Two bodies are lying on the surface of the sea.
 Indira: They are dead!

Cut to.

Scene 78

Location: Cave

Day: Exterior

Characters: Water man- Indira-Whales

Water man and Indira reach to their cave. They get down and tie the boat on the shore with a rope.

They have got injured during the fight.

Camera's Zoom on Indira's face…

   Indira: Tomorrow   morning we will start from here

to an island.

Water man's close up…

Water man: This is my home…I am born and brought up

here; I don't want to go anywhere.

Cut to

Scene 79

Location: Sea

Day: Exterior

Characters: Water man- Indira

Indira's close up…she is convincing him.

Suddenly boat stops…

Mid shot… They are in the middle of the sea.

        Indira: (Panic expression) she moves ahead, turns the key but the boat does not

start..   Water man: What happened? Why it is not working?

She checks the oil tank.

Indira: Oil is over…

They get much panicked as they are now stuck in the middle of the sea.

She gives a thought…and moves to the back of the boat.

She pulls out two wooden sticks and they start throwing the water on the other direction with the help of

the sticks…so boat can move forward.

Scene 80

Location: Sea

Evening: Exterior

Characters: Water man- Indira

Flash cuts of Water man and Indira.

Water man is giving fish to Indira…Indira is shivering with cold.

Voice Over: (Indira) We did not have anything to eat…so we ate raw fish. It

was such a difficult journey. We thought we would never find any island; there was nothing else but water. We spent many days in the sea.

Cut to

Scene 81

Location: Sea

Night: Exterior

Characters: Water man- Indira

Flash cuts of Water man and Indira.

Water man is giving fish to Indira…Indira is shivering with cold.

Voice Over: (Indira) We did not have anything to eat…so we ate raw fish. It was

       such a difficult journey. We thought we would never find any island;

       there was nothing else but water. We spent many days in the sea.

Cut to.

Scene 82

Location: Sea

Night: Exterior

Characters: Water man- Indira

Boat enters in the frame…

Lights are glittering all over …

It's a different world for water man…he cant understand it.

His eyes are incapable of taking the lights in.

Cut to.

Scene 83

Location: Sea Shore

Night: Exterior

Characters: Water man- Indira-Shop keeper

Indira and Water man move out from the boat.

Indira: Water man, you hide in the boat…I will go and get some clothes.

Indira reaches to a clothes shop…all the shop keepers are watching her.

Shop keeper: (In Chinese) How can I help you, madam?

She cannot understand their language and vice-versa.

Indira touches the clothes…and in sign language asks for it.

Shop keeper shows her few clothes.

She buys 2 pair of clothes and walks out.

Cut to

Scene 84

Location: Sea

Night: Exterior

Characters: Water man- Fisher man

A fisher man enters the boat with a torch in his hand. He sees that some strange thing is moving.

(Its Water man)

He puts his torch on him.

Water man runs and jumps into the water.

Fisher man gets scared and runs away from there.

He comes back with many people.

Cut to

Scene 85

Location: Sea Shore

Night: Exterior

Characters: Fisher Man- Frankistain

Dark in the sea…something is lying there.

All the fisher men start throwing stones on him… Everybody is scared.

Terror in the atmosphere….

An image gets up…stretches his hands and roars.

(heavy sound effect)

It's "FRANKISTEIN". His body is full of stitches.

Fisher men get scared and take their steps back.

Then, all of them come forward and attack Frankenstein.

Cut to.

Scene 86

Location: Sea Shore

Night: Exterior

Characters: Fisher Man- Frankistain

Fight between Frankenstein and the fisher men.

Frankenstein kills few men and a few are injured.

Frankenstein too… gets hurt by some swords.

Police siren in the background.

Cut to

Scene 87

Location: Sea Shore

Night: Exterior

Characters: Fisher Man- Frankistain-Police

Police cars enters in the frame…

They see the man (Frankenstein) that looks like a monster. They start firing on him.

Frankenstein runs and disappears in front of their eyes.

Cut to

Scene 88

Location: Sea Shore

Night: Exterior

Characters: Fisher Man- Frankistain-Police

Indira reaches on the shore, holding clothes in her hand. She gets shocked to see the dead and injured people surrounded by the police.

Cut to

Scene 89

Location: Sea Shore

Night: Exterior

Characters: Fisher Man -Police

A police officer comes to her.

Police man: You look like a stranger…where are you from? What are you doing here?

Show me your passport!

Indira: I don't have a passport.

Indira explains everything to them and also tells them about Water man.

Police: Oh…so his name is Water man. Who has killed so many people here? And

run away.

They arrest her and put her into their car.

Indira: Inspector, I know Water man is innocent, let me find him.

Inspector: Madam, whatever you have to say…say in the police station. We are

sorry…we are doing our job; you have to come to the police station.

Cut to

Scene 90

Location: Street

Night: Exterior

Characters: Indira –Water man -Police

3 Police cars are running very fast. Indira is in the middle car.

Water man comes from the top…fights with policemen and takes Indira along.

Cut to

Scene 91

Location: Police Headquater

Day: Interior

Characters: Police Officers

Police Headquater...

In a room, senior police officer is sitting around the table with 4 other officers.

Senior officer: It's a shame for our department. I am giving you 24 hours time to find the person who killed these many lives.

Cut to

Scene 92

Location: Chinese Home

Day: Interior

Characters: Few Chinese People

Shot opens T.V. in the frame.

In a stranger home...few Chinese people are sitting and watching the T.V.

News reader: Today, near the_____ sea, we found a man looking like a monster...he killed 20 people on the spot and 45 are injured. Police are unable to locate from where that monster came. There is this girl with him, *(On the screen Indira's picture)*

Cut to.

Scene 93

Location: Press

Day: Interior

Characters:

Early morning

Newspapers rolling down...

Head line... An alien accompanied by a girl, killed 20 people, near the sea shore.

Cut to

Scene 94

Location: Forest

Day: Exterior

Characters: Indira –Water man

Water man and Indira are running and reach to a forest. (Indira holding the clothes in her hand.)

Indira: Did you kill all the men over there?

Water man: No... I was hiding under the water and I saw a man who killed all.

Indira's reaction.

Indira: I am going to get some food for us. Be careful, all around police are

searching for us.

Water man: You too...be careful.

Indira nods her head.

Cut to.

Scene 95

Location: Shop

Day: Exterior/ Interior

Characters: Indira –Shop keeper- Police car

Indira is on the street...she looks around. A police car passes on the other road.

Indira goes to a shop…almost with covered face. Shopkeeper looks at her suspiciously.

Indira buys some food and sees the newspaper lying on the table.

There is a picture of her…she takes it along.

Cut to.

Scene 96

Location: Forest

Day: Exterior

Characters: Water man-Indira- Police car

Water man and Indira are sitting and eating. Indira shows him the newspaper.

 Indira: The Police are searching all over; we have to go back to the shore, take a

 ship and escape from here. Once we reach India, the police cannot do

 anything to us.

Cut to.

Scene 97

Location: Sea Shore

Night: Exterior

Characters: Water man- Indira- Naval officers

On the sea shore…ship is in the frame…

Water man comes out of the water and jumps in a ship…with a split of a second…he throws the rope, lying in the ship in the water…Indira catches it and starts climbing up.

Some naval security around hears the sound, looks around and comes up to the ship. A barrel is rolling in the ship; they go back on the shore.

Cut to.

Scene 98

Location: Sea

Night: Exterior

Characters: Water man- Indira

Sun light is passing through the ship window…

Camera is outside the window…Indira enters in the frame (out of focus*) and removes the mist from the window, focus is on Indira.* She is surprised and happy.

Outside… far from the ship, she sees a few buildings.

Indira comes up to Water man and shows him the view she is seeing.

   Indira: Water man, we will reach India soon, see that's Mumbai.

We are only few kilometers away from our destination.

Cut to

Scene 99

Location: Street

Morning: Exterior

Characters: Water man- Indira- Police officers

A car is coming towards the camera…

Indira is sitting and Water man is hiding in the corner.

Indira notices from the mirror of the car…a few police men in civil dress are following them.

Cut to

Scene 100

Location: Street

Day : Exterior

Characters: Water man- Indira- William- Ajay-Staff

Arial shot… camera coming down from the top…*some greenish body is moving…*

Camera zoom back…in control room, satellite displays the car with a blood spot on it.

Control room person contacts William.

William with Ajay and two men, are in the helicopter, just above the two cars…are following Water man and Indira.

Police car tries to overtake Indira's car.

Ajay starts firing on Indira's car…it gets hit and rolls down.

Helicopter lands near the car, Indira and Water man are injured, come out of the car.

Police takes Indira and Water man under their custody.

Cut to

Scene 101
Location: Near Forest
Night: Exterior
Characters: Frankiestain- Elephant

A huge image (Frankenstein) comes out of the sea and enters the forest…a helicopter passes from the top. Frankenstein is screaming with pain in his body…he has destroyed so many trees.
An elephant comes in front of him… *Frankenstein fights…kills and starts eating it.*
After eating again he screams out his lungs.

Cut to

Scene 102
Location: Jail
Night: Interior
Characters: Water man- Indira-William- Police

In the jail… , behind the bars..Water man is lying unconscious.
Indira is sitting outside… explaining Water man's innocence to William.
Female police come in between and forcefully take her away from William.
Water man gets conscious and quickly gets up… with anger, he breaks the bars and jumps out, to reach Indira.

Indira is shouting and requesting a man who moves towards Waterman to give him an anesthesia injection.

Cut to

Scene 103
Location: Minister office
Day: Interior
Characters: Minister-William- Police

William is sitting with the minister and is surrounded by the Press…who are asking him about the dragon who killed thousands of people.
William is unable to comment on anything at that moment and for now the press reporters are not allowed to take any pictures of Water man.
William gets a message from his department… that the dragon (Water man) has escaped from the jail.
William gets up and runs towards to control room.

Cut to

Scene 104
Location: Control Room
Day: Interior
Characters: Water man-William- Ajay

In control room…the computer (which is connected to satellite)
displays: Water man is there… 600 km. far from the jail.
William gets shocked to see him.
  Ajay: How is this possible?? Just 10 minutes back we   saw him in the jail!

How can he reach 600 km. in just 10 minutes??

Cut to …

Scene 105

Location: Forest

Day: Exterior

Characters: William- Ajay- Frankeistain-Staff-Tiger

William and Ajay with some of their staff are in the helicopter…they follow the satellite image and reach the forest.

Their helicopter lands and they all come out with a display in Ajay's hand which is connected to satellite and is searching for the dragon (Frankenstein).

While reaching to the location…a tiger attacks one of William's staff, Frankenstein jumps on the tiger from the top of a tree and kills it.

William sees Frankenstein who looks entirely different from Water man, he fires on Frankenstein.

Frankenstein's mouth is full of animal's blood, gets shot and falls near Williams's leg.

With the help of the staff…they keep Frankenstein (in a cage) in the helicopter and fly away.

Cut to

Scene 106

Location: Sea

Day: Exterior

Characters: William- Ajay- Frankeistain-Staff

Helicopter is passing from the sea…suddenly Frankenstein breaks his cage and all the people drown in the sea along with their helicopter.

Cut to.

Scene 107

Location: Sea

Day: Exterior

Characters: William- Ajay- Frankeistain-Staff-Navel officers

A helicopter with naval officers in it, reaches and all the officers jump in the sea to save William, Ajay and other staff.

Frankenstein is missing from there.

Cut to.

Scene 108
News Paper

Camera is on the front page of the newspaper…
Indira's picture is on the cover page…and headline… Water man is missing from jail and has killed 100s of people. This girl called Indira is with him and equally supporting him in all the crime.

Cut to.

Scene 109
Location: William's Cabin
Day: Interior
Characters: Indira-William

William has seen Frankenstein… he remembers the entire thing which Indira explained about Water man.

William (thinks aloud): I think Indira was right, this is not Water man who is committing all the crime but Frankenstein.

William decides to leave Indira from the jail so that she can find Water man and help them in order to kill Frankenstein.

Cut to

Scene 110

Location: Street (Car)

Day: Exterior /Interior

Characters: William- Ajay

William and Ajay are following the satellite display, which is leading them to Frankenstein.

Cut to.

Scene 111

Location: Street (Car)

Day: Exterior/Interior

Characters: Shelly and Dr. Bhishmacharya

With the help of the camera signal, Shelly and Dr. Bhishmacharya reach Frankenstein & fix his right eye….

Cut to.

Scene 112

Location: Street (Car)

Day: Exterior

Characters: William –Ajay-Shelly- Dr. Bhishmacharya

William notices a car following them. They stop and arrest Shelly and Bhismacharya.

Cut to.

Scene 113

Location: Jail

Day: Interior

Characters: William –Ajay-Shelly- Dr. Bhishmacharya

Shelly and Dr. Bhishamacharya… disclose the story about how they created Frankenstein.

Cut to

Scene 114

Location: Indira's Home

Day: Interior

Characters: Indira –Water man-Parents

Indira's parents get scared and inform William to take Water man away from their home.

Indira: Water man, we have to go and find the dragon. Only then, we can survive in

this place.

Cut to

Scene 115

Location: Sea

Day: Exterior

Characters: Indira –Water man-Frankistain

Water man and Indira find (reach to) Frankenstein.

Fight between Water man and Frankenstein.

Cut to

Scene 116

Location: Sea

Day: Exterior

Characters: Indira –Water man-Frankistain-Navel Officers

In the middle of the sea…fight is going on between Water man and Frankenstein.

Naval officers start firing from the helicopter…top of the sea.

Indira: (crying and shouting) Water man please save yourself…I can't live without you. You are going to be father very soon.

Few bullets go in to Water man's body too. Under water fight between Water man and Frankenstein …so many Whales are around them to support Water man.

Cut to
Scene 117
Location: Sea/ Helicopter
Day: Exterior
Characters: Indira –Water man-Frankistain-William-Navel Officers

William is watching them in the monitor through the satellite. Water Man is injured badly and unable to fight Frankenstein anymore.

Cut to

Scene 118
Location: Sea
Day: Exterior
Characters: Indira –Water man-Frankistain-William-Navel Officers

On the top of the sea, in the sky…, William throws a rope down from the helicopter. Indira tries to catch the rope but her hand slips off. Frankenstein comes out from the water with heavy sound in the Background… he takes her and throws her far into the sea. Indira sinks deep down in the sea.
Water man is injured; he comes out of the water, and tries to save Indira…meanwhile Frankenstein attacks on Water man.
Water man defends himself and comes out of the water with
Indira.
Indira is unconscious… Water man takes out all the water from her.
Indira regains consciousness.

Cut to

Scene 119
Location: Sea
Day: Exterior
Characters: Indira –Water man-Frankistain-William-Navel Officers

Sound of Bullets appears in the background…Water man turns… Frankenstein is standing behind him.
William is firing on Frankenstein from the Helicopter… Frankenstein gets injured and runs from
there.
Helicopter lands down and William takes Indira with
him.
Indira doesn't want to leave Water man alone… she is crying …Water man is also helpless… Slowly
helicopter flies away from Waterman… leaves him behind.
Frankenstein comes to Water man and attacks him. Heavy fight between Frankenstein and Water
man.

Cut to

Scene 120
Location: Sea
Day: Exterior
Characters: Indira –William-Navel Officers

Water man and Frankenstein have disappeared in the water. The only thing William can see is a whale.
William takes Indira away from there.

Cut to

Scene 121
Location: Micro phone cabin
Night time: Interior
Characters: Water girl- Indira-Shelly- William

76

Present

Old Indira is weeping…

William is standing near her… he moves towards Indira.

      William: I will tell you … what happened after that.

Cut to

Scene 122

Location: Micro phone cabin

Night time: Interior

Characters: Water girl- Indira-Shelly- William

William finds… Water man and Frankenstein have been eaten by the sharks around.

They close the case.

Cut to

Scene 123

Location: Micro phone cabin

Night time: Interior

Characters: Water girl- Indira-Shelly- William

Shelly and Dr. Bhishmacharya get life time imprisonment for creating unnatural creation against Indian medical law….

In the jail…Bhishmacharya commits suicide…

and Williams gets promotion from his department.

Cut to

Scene 124

Location: Hospital

Night time: Interior

Characters: Indira- William-Doctor

Indira has lost her memory…

The doctor tells Williams that she is unable to speak and … now she can't remember anything.

Doctor: Indira remembers only the last thing she saw…Water man got killed by Frankenstein. It was indeed a big shock for her, she is unable to get out of it. She is carrying an unnatural creature in her womb. We don't have enough technology for this kind of a patient. To save her and her child's life, we have to send her to France.

William: I and my department are ready for any kind of help you need for her treatment.

Cut to

Scene 123

Location: Micro phone cabin

Night time: Interior

Characters: Water girl- Indira-Shelly- William

 flash back.. return back….

Indira is confused and asks him: How do u know about all this? William: Not only me. .. sitting in front of you… this lady… her real name is Mary Shelly…but for last 20 years she is living as Shelly… you must have read about her. Shelly is taking care of your child for past 20 years because she repents what she has done unknowingly to your life.

Indira to Shelly: Whatever happened I don't want to hear, you have taken care of my child for years… that's enough for me.

And she hugs Shelly.

Cut to

Scene 124

Location: Water girl cabin

Night time: Interior

Characters: Water girl- Frankistain- Water man

In Water girl's cabin… nurse arrange the things so that Water girl can sleep comfortably…nurse says good night…switches off the light and leaves.

Cut to

Scene 125
Location: Shelly's cabin
Night time: Interior
Characters: Shelly

Shelly is seeing her in the monitor; she switches of the light and goes to sleep in her room.

Cut to

Scene 126
Location: Indira's home
Day time: Interior
Characters: Indira

Indira is sitting in front of her the computer.
She starts searching through all the journal news paper and photographs and finds…
Rewarded young Williams …. 20 years back…
   Indira: (Thinks aloud) William was Vijay Shastri… but why has he changed his

  name… there is something secret behind this!
She turnes the page…

Headline: Frankenstein killed by Water man… Bhishamacharya who had created Frankenstein killed himself. Frankenstein was Dr. Marry Shelly's love.

All Flash Cuts.

Suddenly, there is a glass breaking sound in the background… a shadow enters. Some footsteps are heard in the background.

Indira thinks that the computer is making that noise.

The s*hadow is moving ahead and stands close to Indira.*

Shadow moves its hand…it looks like Williams hand and touches her face.

Indira gets scared; she closes her eyes and starts shouting out her lungs. (In the background, dogs are barking loudly)

Shadow turns back and stands near the broken window.

Indira opens her eyes and looks at the shadow with fear.

   Indira : Who are you? Why you come here?

Indira picks up the remote and switches on the light.

Shadow turns to her…

Shadow: Indira, I am your Water man; I have come here for you.

     Indira: No….this is not possible! He died in front of my eyes. Remove that cover

from your head …I want to see your face.

Water man: I am badly injured… you will not be able to see my face, but I will remove

the cover from my head if you insist.

*Water man takes off his head cover…*one side of his face is wounded…full of blood & the other side is burnt.

Indira sees into his eyes… which she can easily recognize.

*Indira starts crying…*to see him in this condition, *she moves to him and hugs him.*

Water man: I searched for you… all over the world; these wounds are the gifts of the

people.

     Indira: Our daughter is also here, come I will take you to her.

Indira and Water man move towards Water girl's cabin.

Cut to

Scene 127

Location: Micro phone cabin

Night time: Interior

Characters: Water girl- Shelly- William-Frankistain

Water girl's room is full of mess... two security guards' bodies lie dead on the floor.

Frankenstein is standing near Water girl's tub…holding a gun in his hand, blood is dripping down from his body, his one leg is broken, *he is crying with pain.*

William and Shelly are standing opposite to him with terror on their face.

Frankenstein: I am looking for Water man, He is responsible for all the things I have been through, he is going to pay for it. Shelly…you have created me; I was looking for you for long… now I want you to create my pair… I am living alone for many years. Till the time you create my pair, I will take Water girl along…if anybody tries to follow me, I will kill Water girl and everybody around.

William accepts Frankenstein's talk to save Water girl.

Shelly: Please don't kill anybody… I can't accept your demand

Scene 128

Location: Street

Night time: Exterior

Characters: Shelly

Scene opens with a very wide road... hardly anybody is there... In the midnight, Shelly is driving the car, she sees a shadow crossing her way, she stops.

Reverses her car, searches for the thing she sees, but nothing is there. But she feel something strange is following her.

Shelly calls the senior Dr. and asks: Is Water girl fine? Tighten the security for her.

cut to

Scene 129

Location: Sea

Night time: Exterior

Characters:

In the dark midnight... it's raining. There is thunder & lightening falls down in the sea (with thundering light we reveal its sea) camera travels in the water with lightening which becomes cyclone... and bubbles comes out on the surface of the sea... like somebody is breathing. An image comes out of cyclone and travels deep in with lightening.

Cut to

Scene 130

Location: Water girl Tank

Night time: Interior

Characters: Water girl

All the cables which were connected to Water girl's body are lying down on the ground. The water level of the Water tank starts getting lower and lower.

Slowing all the water moves out of tank.

One hand comes up on the glass window...Camera pan down... glass is broken down. (Water girl   is kidnapped by Frankenstein).

Cut to

Scene 131

Location: Water girl Tank

Night time: Interior

Characters: Water girl

One hand... (which does not seem like human hand) comes in from the window and throws a cable in... the cable somehow was still attached to Water girl's body. One by one when all the cables start getting removed from Water girl's body... siren starts ringing to alert the security.

Cut to

Scene 132

Location: Street

Night time: Exterior

Characters: Shelly

Shelly is driving... with a sudden jerk, she stops. She gets the alert message of Water girl being kidnapped.

Cut to

Scene 133

Location: Water girl Tank

Night time: Interior

Characters: Water girl-William-Ajay-Staff

Camera (study cam) is on Water girl's tank... it moves back...robots which have the screen on their backs are scanning all the things and trying to find the evidence.
William lifts the broken glass and finds some finger prints on it.
William moves the glass from opposite his face....*camera zooms in...* he thinks of something and gives order to his crew to get ready and move to find Water girl.

Cut to

Scene 134

Location: Alps Mountain/ Himalaya

Night time: Exterior

Characters: William-Ajay-Staff

Camera is in the helicopter... *from top angle...search lights on arrival view...Long shot* of William and crew.

Mountains are covered with mist and fog... search lights are travelling all over the place.

Helicopter comes down to land. *(Suggestion of helicopter's wings moving ...audio effect and storm graphics)*

Cut to

Scene 135

Location: Alps Mountain/ Himalaya

Night time: Exterior

Characters: William-Ajay-Staff

Wide shot of mountains which is full of mist and snow... landing of the helicopter.

William, Ajay and crew get down with packed bags of paragliding, They have search light belts on their heads and all the possible gear needed, to search for Water girl.

Wide scene of the mountain with mist and snow.

Cut to

Scene 136

Location: Alps Mountain/ Himalaya

Night time: Exterior

Characters: William-Ajay-Staff

WILLIAMS AND AJAY FALLING FROM THE VALLEY.....

Thunder fall with lightening.

Cut to

Scene 137

Location: Alps Mountain/ Himalaya

Night time: Exterior

Characters: Two Stars(EFX- Graphics)

Two stars falling slowly towards the land [top of mountain]… gradually lights…. become search lights
and   show the image of two parachutes falling behind the trees;
one comes to camera and blocks the lens.

Cut to

Scene 138

Location: Alps Mountain/ Himalaya

Night time: Exterior

Characters: Terrorist

Frame entry with two barrels of the carbon gun, leather Fur trench, hands covered with gloves.
*One hand moves ahead and opens the door covered with a white layer of snow. Yellow light peeps out
on their faces..*
They enter in and close the door.
In the corner of the room... fire is burning to keep the room warm. (few terrorists are there)

          Leader: I have the entire plan... how I am going to do this.
I will show the world that I am capable of doing anything.
After destroying the Tajmahal which is one of world's seven wonders, world will never forget me...I will
never let Indians be in peace.
He opens up the laptop...Tajmahal's picture is there...camera zoom in...to real Tajmahal...gets blasted.

Cut to

Scene 139

Location: Alps Mountain/ Himalaya

Night time: Exterior

Characters: Frankistain

Entry OF-FRANKEINSTEIN....

Background tourists.... snow covered tent....from the sky one image is coming down...with glitter in its eyes, it lands on ice berg.

Comes on the top...image shatters the ice and half of the body goes in. (Its landing makes an earthquake).

Cut to

Scene 140

Location: Alps Mountain/ Himalaya

Night time: Exterior

Characters: Terrorist

The door of the Terrorist's tent, breaks down...they all come out to...with terror in their eyes.

They start firing on it(Frankenstein). He turns his face to them and changes the way of the bullets coming to him to slow motion. He gets some scratches on his hand and face. Big plastic bags rolled down from his hand.

Frankenstein tries to lift his body from the ice...he comes up with his body surrounded by the layer of ice. He spins up in the air and terrorists fire heavy bullets on him. This breaks the ice that was surrounding his body into millions of pieces which scatter up in the air.

Frankenstein spins again in the air with the broken ice pieces.

Cut to

Scene 141

Location: Alps Mountain/ Himalaya

Night time: Exterior

Characters: Frankistain

Frankenstein...spins up and catches a tree branch to keep him steady.

O.S. of Frankenstein... terrorists are still firing in the air and looking all around to find him (Frankenstein).

Cut to

Scene 142

Location: River

Night time: Exterior

Characters: Terrorist

Camera is on low angle... plastic cover is rolling down towards the camera. While rolling, one arm comes out ...full of blood ... and falls in the river (in slow motion)...and bubbles come out.   In a split of second...one man (Ajay) falls down with his parachute; which has broken down from the bullet of terrorist when they were firing on Frankenstein...opposite the river. Ajay gets up, tries to remove the parachute belt...suddenly a body falls down in the water which is of William. After 30 secs., parachute falls and floats on the water.

Cut to

Scene 143

Location: Valley

Night time: Exterior

Characters: William-Ajay

Ajay is holding onto the parachute which is hanging from the tree...he looks up and searches for William...he cant find him and then looks around to see William's parachute floating on the water... he opens the parachute belt, jumps down and runs to save him...William is struggling under the water to come out (he cant swim).

A wide angle...Ajay is running towards river to take William out of water...and he jumps in.

Cut to

Scene 144
Location: Valley
Night time: Exterior
Characters: William-Ajay

Ajay is at   the riverside… he detaches the parachute from his body.   He
searches for William…
he had seen Williams para balloon on top of the water..
he jumps in the water for Williams.

Cut to….

Scene 145
Location: Under water
Night time: Interior
Characters: Water man -Whale

Camera is in the water…from far away…. a huge whale is coming towards the camera.
It moves up towards the surface of the water…a man (Water man) is riding it like horse… holding its ears
(gills).
Comes up on the surface of the water in slow motion…(180 degree camera movement + EFX)

Cut to

Scene 146
Location: Sky (Ariel View)
Night time: Exterior
Characters: Water man -Whale

the ariel view …

Camera is in the helicopter... water man comes towards the cloud with the jumping power of the whale...

towards the lens of the camera, bottom sea level...and the whale is diving from the air to the water

Cut to

Scene 147
Location: Sea
Night time: Exterior
Characters: Water man -Whale

Wide angle....camera is on the sea level...whale comes up on the air...jumps back in the water.... water splashes like a fountain..

on the suggestion of water... Water man lands before the snowy mountain.

Cut to.

Scene 148
Location: Sky (Ariel View)
Night time: Exterior
Characters: Frankistain

Dark wide long shot...all the trees are standing straight...in between those trees, one tree is bow shaped.

Close up of Frankenstein.........he is trying to listen to some sound...the branch of the tree he was hanging on...is about to break.

Cut to

Scene 149
Location: valley
Morning: Exterior
Characters: Frankistain-William- ajay

*Camera is on the level of the sea...*William and Ajay come out of the river...in front of them a tree falls down.. They pull out their guns and start firing...With the sound of firing, Frankenstein lands from the tree and hides.

William and Ajay notice a few dead bodies of terrorists lying near the river and they also notice the evidence of Water girl being nearby.

Ajay: Terrorists must have kidnapped Water girl from the lab.

William: She is a gracious miracle to this world...we have to find her, *(thinking seriously)* I think she is in the river and if so, she can't survive in this chilling water.

After giving a thought, Ajay jumps back in the river and start searching for Water girl. William stands on the shore feeling reckless.

Cut to….

Scene 150
Location: Valley
Morning: Exterior
Characters: William-Ajay-Water girl-Shelly

Camera is in the helicopter… from top view…William and Ajay are sitting near the lake….they burn a fire to warm Water girl.

Helicopter lands on the bank of the river…Shelly and the senior Dr. come down and walk towards Water girl. Shelly sits near Water girl…starts treating her with the help of senior Dr.

Another helicopter comes…in the background water girl is getting treatment…foreground… a shadow comes down from the helicopter (out of focus), focus shifts…its Water girl's incubator…

They shift Water girl to incubator, keep the incubator in the (white color) helicopter.

The rest of the staff shifts to another helicopter (blue color).

Cut to

Scene 151

Location: Valley

Day time: Exterior

Characters: Frankistain

Both the helicopters take off with a heavy sound in the background.

Cut to

Scene 152

Location: Sky (Trees)

Day time: Exterior

Characters: Frankistain-Helicopter

It passes by the tree where Frankenstein is hiding…he jumps over from one tree to another to catch the (white) helicopter…somehow he slips and catches the another (blue) helicopter

Cut to

Scene 153

Location: Forest (near the Sea)

Day time: Exterior

Characters: Frankistain- Helicopter

With the weight of Frankenstein, the helicopter slops down and moves out of frame. *[build up]EFX,CROMA]MINIATURE ;*

BUT THE OTHER HELECOPTER goes away from this one..

… The other helicopter with Water girl in it flies away.

Cut to.

Scene 154
Location: Sea
Day time: Exterior
Characters: Waterman-Frankistain-Helicopter

In the long shot…Alps behind the sea…white helicopter flies away and the other is slopping down towards the sea.

Cut to..

Scene 155
Location: Sea
Day time: Exterior
Characters: Water man-Frankistain-Helicopter

Water man is on the top of the hills…turns in slow motion…sees Frankenstein going down in the sea. Water man's reaction…cut to…Many flash backs of 20 years back, from water man's point of view.

Cut to

Scene 156
Location: Sea
Day time: Exterior
Characters: Frankistain-Helicopter

From long shot to zoom in….Frankenstein will enter in the frame holding the front of the helicopter…gradually he goes under the water, then the helicopter.

Cut to

Scene 157

Location: Sea

Day time: Exterior

Characters: Water man-Frankistain-

Water man's reaction…and he disappears from there.

Cut to

Scene 158

Location: Sea (under Water)

Day time: Exterior

Characters: Frankistain-Whales – Militry Staff Helicopter

Under water…Wale's suggestion… Frankistain is moving down in the water and helicopter is sinking too.

Cut to

Scene 159

Location: Sea

Day time: Exterior

Characters: Water man-Frankistain-Helicopter

Under the water…helicopter gets hits a big rock and crashes into the pieces.

All the staff dies and there bodies come up on the surface of the water.

Cut to

Scene 160

Location: Sea

Day time: Exterior

Characters: Frankistain-Whales

*Camera under the water…*Frankenstein is surrounded by around 20 whales….visualization of 20 whale attacks on Frankenstein…

*Camera on the top…*water is moving(fight between Frankenstein and whales)…Blood spreads on the top of the sea.

After 3 seconds silence…

One whale comes up and fall upside down…dies. One after the another, all whales come up, die. Frankenstein comes up spinning…and fall on the other side of water and disappears.

Cut to...

Scene 161

Location: Snowy Mountain

Day time: Exterior

Characters: Water man-Terriost

STEADY CAME MOVMENT OF THE SNOWY MOUNTAIN FORE GROUND.

Camera following the violet color liquid....

camera stays in front of the river...

During the fight, the terrorists that are hidden in the caves, come out. They are all carrying their carbon guns and missile parts on their shoulders.

They are examining the place…(leader is standing in the center).

They find that some danger is coming towards them.

Leader: Before anything unwanted comes, I will have to finish my work.

He opens his laptop and fixes the time (5 minutes) to destroy the Tajmahal. On his computer display… countdown starts from 04:55:00, he talks on the wireless phone.

Cut to

Scene 162

Location: Taj Mahal

Day time: Exterior

Characters: Terriost- guide

Scene opens in front of the Tajmahal…with tourists. Guide disconnects the phone. He removes the battery and sim card.

All foreigner visitors are around him…he is explaining the history of Tajmahal.

Reaction of the tourists.

(They all are wearing plastic shoes cover provided by the security of Tajmahal)

While explaining…they are heading towards the interior of Tajmahal. Meanwhile, one child is there with a tourist. Guide gets a soft corner towards the child. Now he does not want him to die and tries to keep them all away from the Tajmahal, even though he doesn't know them all.

Close up of their there legs moving towards death.

They all reach to security check…guide's *close up with the terror of death in his eyes.*

While going through the security check…every one hears the beep.

Suddenly… Guide himself shouts,"Everyone… please move from here, I am holding a bomb with me. I don't want anyone to die."

Cut to

Scene 163

Location: Taj Mahal

Day time: Exterior

Characters: Water man-Tourist-Security Guards

Terror in the atmosphere…all of them try to run from there…and lie on the floor, closing their eyes.

Water man lands down from the pillar of the Tajmahal. *(time lapse)* Beep sound becomes more clear and than dissolves. On the top of the Yamuna river one blast. *Water man falls under the water.*

Cut to

Scene 164
Location: Valley
Day time: Exterior
Characters: Terriost

Willam and Ajay came back in the search of the missing helicopter….
Laptop lying open in the snow, displays… operation succeeded. Beside the laptop, they see some dead bodies of terrorists, including their leader. Their faces is covered with violet blue liquid.
Ajay gives an understanding look to William.
Williams reaction (as he knows the fact, this done by whom).
  Cut to

Scene 165
Location: William's Office
Day time: Exterior
Characters: William- CM- Governer

William gets all the credit for destroying the terrorists' plan… he gets an award from the police department.

Cut to

Scene 166
Location: Indira's home
Day time: Interior
Characters: Indira-Water girl-Shelly

After reading the newspaper,   Indira keeps it on the table and thinks aloud…this can't be somebody else but my love, my daughter's father…"Waterman".

Reaction of Watergirl and Shelly.

Cut to

 Water man comes to know about Indira and reaches to meet her and his daughter.

Water man along with Indira reaches to HUMA lab to see Water girl. Frankistain destroyed everything in the lab, taken Water girl along and hidden in the Alps… and demanding to create a female Frankeistain for him, than only he will leave Water girl alive.

Water man reaches to the Alps with the military force… they are searching for Water girl… Frankeistain appears and destroy all the force, William, Indira, shelly with Ajay in the helicopter… Frankeistain attacks on helicopter and it slops down in the water. William with all the person in it…jumps out…and hanged on the top of the tree.

Water man attacks on Frankeistain… heavy fight between them.

Water man lost all his weapon during the fight… he made some sound to call all the animals… a group of white wolf come to help Water man…Frankeistain disappear…from there after seeing the animals, who were about to attack on him.

Water man reaches to help William and all… to land safe on the ground.

Frankistain attacks on him once more… Water man sees Water girl hanging on the top of the hill with the support of thin ice layer which could break any time.

Ice broke and Water girl start sliding down… on the top from the helicopter one hand (Ajay) comes out and saved Water girl.

Frankeistain attacks on the helicopter and throws Ajay out of it… Water man comes in between and attacks on Frankeistain.

While fighting… for saving Water girl from Frankeistain… Shelly lost her life.

Water girl got saved and handed over to Indira.

Under water fight between Water man and Frankeistain… on the top of the water layer, Frankeistains body comes out in so many pieces… Water man is inside the water… he died or alive… nobody knows.

END

BY WINS DEUS

I am an artist, writer, film actor, and director with more than 25 years of experience in the entertainment sector.As a screenwriter, I worked on various Dracula series; in 2005 and 2007, modified and adapted from Bram Stoker's Dracula, which became my well-known TV show during 2005 and 2007 in South India. Ref. Dracula in popular culture was my title as Wins Deus; my actual name is Wins ds,[Devadasan Sasikala Wins] and the second name meaning is translated to achieve the same sound as ds / in Latin Deus.I have created numerous paintings, sculptures, and graphic designs, and I have made my first documentary feature in January 2013 in Hollywood, US. It took many years to complete this project, and it will soon be released online and in film festivals. I haven't had the opportunity to secure funding for my screenplays; I primarily worked on them 10 to 20 years ago, and they all focus on futuristic themes. Some of my investors didn't understand that work, but now it is almost happening as I envision with my screenplays and concepts about 2020-2030.My first screenplay was Dracula, followed by Jesus, Water Man, Moon Man, The Good, The Bad, and The Beauty, The Miracle, The Future, The Cinema, Wings of Will, Vampire Rawhide, Moon Man Dracula, and Hercules Man with a Magic Soul, which was completed in 2009. Many investors read it, and I distributed copies, but after several years, no one was ready to produce it in 2009-2010.After a lengthy wait, I decided that I must publish my screenplays. It's time to achieve auspiciousness to realize some visions.

As an artist, I have produced paintings, sculptures, and installations, as well as collaborated with other artists and designers on projects such as murals, posters, and film prosthetics. My artistic style is eclectic and innovative, merging different mediums and techniques to create distinctive and engaging visuals. My paintings feature mythological and fantasy figures influenced by Shakespeare's works, such as Hamlet, Macbeth, and A Midsummer Night's Dream. I also depict nature scenes that celebrate the beauty and variety of our planet, capturing everything from towering mountains to peaceful lakes. My artwork reflects my fascination with American culture and traditional farming, showcasing the lives and customs of rural communities and their bond with the land. Ultimately, I explore futuristic artistry that imagines the potential and obstacles of the future, touching on themes like artificial intelligence, space exploration, and environmental concerns.I have completed my education at the college of fine arts, in Kerala, where I worked on numerous television documentaries and films for Doordarshan, Asianet, Surya TV, Gemini TV, etc. I have engaged in cinematography, served as a cinematographer, and studied stereography in , USA.

       I am currently focusing on my art and completing some of my unfinished screenplays while residing in Los Angeles , New York, and I often spend a considerable amount of time in Europe, the Himalayas, Ooty, Kodaikanal, and the UAE for my research and life experience. I am the eldest son of Mr. K. Devadasan, a former military member and an award-winning gold medalist from the Prime Minister of India, Indira Gandhi. My mother, D. Sasikala, has also received awards from the Chief Minister of Kerala,. Mr. R. Sankar, the former Chief Minister of Kerala, is her father's cousin brother. I am closely related to Sri Narayana Guru, the social reformer and monk of India.

Wins Deus.